PRAISE F
BEST-SELLI

"Time travel, ancient legends, and seductive romance are seamlessly interwoven into one captivating package."
–*Publishers Weekly* on Midnight's Master

"Dark, sexy, magical. When I want to indulge in a sizzling fantasy adventure, I read Donna Grant."
–Allison Brennan, *New York Times* bestseller

5 Stars! Top Pick! "An absolute must read! From beginning to end, it's an incredible ride."
–*Night Owl Reviews*

"It's good vs. evil Druid in the next installment of Grant's Dark Warrior series. The stakes get higher as discerning one's true loyalties become harder. Grant's compelling characters and continued presence of previous protagonists are key reasons why these books are so gripping. Another exciting and thrilling chapter!"
–*RT Book Reviews* on Midnight's Lover

"Donna Grant has given the paranormal genre a burst of fresh air..."
–*San Francisco Book Review*

Don't miss these other spellbinding novels by

DONNA GRANT

REAPERS

Dark Alpha's Claim
Dark Alpha's Embrace
Dark Alpha's Demand
Dark Alpha's Lover
Tall Dark Deadly Alpha Bundle (1-3)
Coming Soon
Dark Alpha's Night
Dark Alpha's Hunger

DARK KINGS

Dark Heat
Darkest Flame
Fire Rising
Burning Desire
Hot Blooded
Night's Blaze
Soul Scorched
Dragon King (novella)
Passion Ignites
Smoldering Hunger
Smoke and Fire
Dragon Fever (novella)
Firestorm
Blaze
Dragon Burn
Heat
Coming Soon
Torched
Dragon Night (novella)
Dragonfire

DARK WARRIORS
Midnight's Master
Midnight's Lover
Midnight's Seduction
Midnight's Warrior
Midnight's Kiss
Midnight's Captive
Midnight's Temptation
Midnight's Promise
Midnight's Surrender (novella)
Dark Warrior Box Set

DARK SWORD
Dangerous Highlander
Forbidden Highlander
Wicked Highlander
Untamed Highlander
Shadow Highlander
Darkest Highlander
Dark Sword Box Set

ALSO AVAILABLE
Dragon King Coloring Book

Sons of Texas Series
The Hero
The Protector
The Legend

Rogues of Scotland Series
The Craving
The Hunger
The Tempted
The Seduced

Chiasson Series
Wild Fever
Wild Dream
Wild Need
Wild Flame

LaRue Series
Moon Kissed
Moon Thrall
Moon Struck

Shield Series
A Dark Guardian
A Kind of Magic
A Dark Seduction
A Forbidden Temptation
A Warrior's Heart

Druids Glen Series
Highland Mist
Highland Nights
Highland Dawn
Highland Fires
Highland Magic
Dragonfyre

Sisters of Magic Trilogy
Shadow Magic
Echoes of Magic
Dangerous Magic

CONSTANTINE: A HISTORY PART 2

THE DARK KINGS

DONNA GRANT

This is a work of fiction. All of the characters, organizations, and events portrayed in this novel are either products of the author's imagination or are used fictitiously.

ISBN 13: 978-1942017424

www.DonnaGrant.com
www.MotherofDragonsBooks.com

Available in ebook and print editions.

Dear Reader,

Constantine.

Anytime I write the King of Dragon King's name or even mention him, I'm flooded with messages and emails. It truly warms my heart how much everyone is enamored with him.

Whether you're in the I love Con camp, or the I hate Con camp, the simple fact is, everyone wants to know more about this enigmatic leader—myself included.

Since I don't plot my books, I'm forever shocked, excited, overwhelmed, and worried about my characters. Some more than others. And Con has definitely been in that "I'm really troubled about him" category.

There are some books that, when I finish, I sit back and smile at the things the King of Kings has done, happy with his decisions.

Other times, by the time I write The End, I'm anxious to return to the next book to figure out what the hell Con was thinking.

I know I'm not alone in this because of the emails and messages you send. Trust me, I get exactly where you're coming from. The thing is, I'm writing so far ahead of all of you that, sometimes, I forget what has happened. Worse is when I know there's something really big coming and I can't tell you because it'll spoil things.

That's when I tell my kids, who could honestly care less. And even my animals. Though, I do have to say, I truly believe Sisko, my dog, is quite intrigued about everything. ;)

I was asked some time ago if Con would get his own book, which, of course he will. The next question was when? For those who missed that live video, his book will be last. And I even have the date—October 2020.

Now, before you ask if this is the end of the Dragon Kings, I can tell you it'll be the end of this storyline. I have plans for another spinoff. ::evil grin::

But that information is for much later. Now, we're talking about Con. Since you know he's getting a book, I know you all want to know who his heroine is. I will admit for many, many, many books, I didn't know who that might be. I do now. I see the scene in my head.

Just as I see the scene that replays about once a day of when we get to find out who Rhi's Dragon King is. I have no idea when that'll happen, but I'm guessing it'll be sometime in books 15 – 18. I know it's not book 14 because I just wrote and turned that story in.

And how can I talk about Con without Death aka Erith aka Blossom Engel aka Heather aka...well, you'll find out in the story. ;) Death is one of those characters who grabs you from the moment she steps onto the page. She's powerful without being showy, strong without throwing it in your face. And she's got a past that is one humdinger (more on that in the Reaper books. And trust me, you won't want to miss out on it!).

For all of that, she's taken an interest in Con because she knows what he's going through—and what is to come for him. She understands and wants to tell him that without giving away who she is.

Her first visit was what changed Con without him even knowing it. From the moment she gave him the dragon head cufflinks, he hasn't been without them. Those weren't the only gift she gave him, however. In this story, you'll discover what she leaves behind on this visit.

So, once more, let us delve into another behind-the-scenes moment with our favorite King of Golds to find out what makes Con tick. It's time, my dedicated dragon lovers, to see yet another side of him.

And maybe, just maybe, by peeling away the armor he's so carefully constructed, we might discover some secrets.

With much love,

DG

TABLE OF CONTENTS

The 20th of April, human year 1746 Dreagan

I have tried. I truly have. Some might look back and say that I didn't give it enough, but I will know the truth.

The simple fact is, the mortals have lost their bloody minds.

I knew it was a good idea to have a spy in the English parliament long before Culloden, and Keltan has done a fine job relaying information while keeping his true identity a secret. But learning that the English plan to pass The Dress Act in the next few months that would make wearing a tartan or kilt illegal leaves me flummoxed. And fuming.

Some of the Kings wish to use our magic to stop such idiocy, but we won't. Just as we didn't intervene or participate in Culloden or the many other battles before that—or the ones yet to come. We have chosen to live among—but apart from—the humans.

And for very good reason.

It is impossible to look at the mortals without disdain for their stupidity or respect for their accomplishments. Thankfully, the spell I cast prevents such deep emotions within the Kings in regards to the humans. Otherwise, I'm not sure even I could keep from eradicating them.

The years are a blur. They pass as quickly as sand through my fingers.

Worse yet, is that my brethren are terribly, enormously lonely. It's an ache experienced by all. Each attempts to hide it, but it's there in their gaze, in their words, and in the very things they do not say.

And, if I'm being honest, I'm lonely, too.

I will never admit it to anyone. It's difficult enough to divulge it in this journal. It's a secret I keep concealed, because if I let it show, if I concede that I feel such emotions, then it's a weakness that can—and will—be used against me by our enemies.

The Fae Wars might be over, and we may be

on friendly terms with the Light, but I know the Dark Fae will never give up in their quest to take over this realm. It's a prime hunting ground for them. They will always be adversaries. And they're patient enough to wait to strike at the best moment.

Then there's Ulrik.

He wants to challenge me. Perhaps, he'll win. Perhaps he won't.

I try to prepare for all these things. I know they're coming. It's a feeling deep within me, like a warning bell. Just as I know that our power, our magic, will draw other enemies to us. Will we be ready?

We have to be. We've lost too much already. I will not allow anyone to take what we've fought so hard to maintain after everything we've given up.

I owe it to the other Kings to ensure that. And I will. Even if it means I forfeit my life. Because, in the end, I am merely one dragon. Any of the other Kings could take my place—even Ulrik. But they are the ones who are important. The dragons are gone from this realm, but the Dragon Kings must remain at all costs.

Constantine, the King of Golds
King of Dragon Kings

Con stared at the words in his journal for a long moment before he slowly closed the book and tied the strip of leather that held it closed. He then placed his hand over the smooth cover and sat back in the chair before his desk.

In his chamber were shelves of other journals—and one hidden. He didn't remember when he began penning his thoughts. It wasn't necessary, but doing it allowed him to write down his troubles to better get a handle on things.

He also found that by detailing his struggles or worries, he sometimes found answers he hadn't thought about before. The real benefit of putting his thoughts on paper was that it permitted him to clear his mind—even if only for a moment or two.

The uncertainties...the doubt was always there. Like shadows that grew each day. How long before they overwhelmed him? Before they consumed him?

Shakespeare had it right when he said that "uneasy lies the head that wears a crown."

Con missed his chats with William. The playwright had a wicked sense of humor and an easy nature. He'd never pried into Con's life. Perhaps that's why Con had enjoyed talking to Shakespeare.

With a sigh, Con rubbed his forehead. He could sit there all night thinking of the few mortals that he'd met and liked, even admired. But they were all gone now. In a blink, a human was born and then died. Some did great things with the little time they had, but most threw their opportunities away. Or squandered them.

Con looked down at the dragon head cufflinks at his wrists. Heather. He'd never forget her name. Yet, he couldn't pull her image from memory. It was one of the reasons he'd drawn her right after she'd drifted through Dreagan like a summer breeze only to disappear.

He'd looked for her for decades, without any luck. Each time he ventured from Dreagan, he found himself searching for her.

There wasn't a day that went by that he didn't think of her whenever he put on the cufflinks.

Heather had understood him as only one other ever had. If only he knew where she was. Or *what* she was. Because he was convinced that she wasn't mortal. Nor was she Fae. The cufflinks had no magic within them.

Yet there was something about the lovely, amiable Heather that intrigued him. He wanted to find her and thank her for her present.

He turned his wrist and looked at the gold dragon head. He could count on one hand the number of times he'd been given a gift. Which was one reason she stood out in his mind.

Her disappearance was another.

Con glanced at his journal. He should go to his chamber and find the one that held his sketch of her to help him remember. Not that he ever expected to find her. He leaned his head back and smiled. He didn't need to recall her face to remember the kindness she'd shown him.

He sat there for another half hour before he extinguished the candle and rose from the desk. It was another few hours before it was his turn to patrol. He walked from his office and along the corridor to the stairs.

The manor was quiet. Too quiet for a home of so many Dragon Kings. Only a handful was awake at the moment. The others were in their mountains, sleeping. He wondered if there would ever be a time when the manor overflowed with noise and Kings again.

In fact, he hoped it didn't. He'd much rather leave it all behind to be a dragon, never shifting into human form again. It was a dream he held onto as tightly as the other one.

The dream he didn't speak of, the one he hid beneath layers of stone walls, it was one he physically ached to have come true. He tried not to think about it. Because that dream broke his heart all over again.

With his mood now melancholy, he made his way out of the manor and headed toward the Dragonwood. There wasn't a part of Dreagan that he didn't love. Every inch of it was special to him. From the moment he hatched, he'd felt the pull of it because the magic was so dazzling, so strong.

So luminous.

Once in the trees, Con drew in a deep breath and released it. The Dragonwood was unique. For within the trees beat the heart of magic. While he felt the power all over Dreagan, even in the mountain connected to the manor, it was distinctive within the forest.

Each night before he patrolled, he walked the woods. There was no particular direction he took. He let his feet lead him. Con had only been in the Dragonwood for a few minutes when he felt someone break the barrier of magic that surrounded Dreagan.

And it was close to him.

"I'm checking it," he told the other Kings through their mental link.

Con shifted directions and headed to the point where their barrier had been breached. He looked through the thick foliage as he reached the stream. Movement ahead slowed his steps. So many animals crossed the invisible wall that they'd made adjustments to the magic so only people or objects would alert them to an intruder.

He came to a halt when he saw the woman standing at the edge of the water, watching the stream. Con took in the red, black, and yellow tartan arisaid, or cloak that extended from her shoulders to her heels. A metal brooch fastened the arisaid above her breasts, and a leather belt cinched it at her waist. She, like many Scottish women, used the arisaid as a head covering, as well, making it impossible for him to see the color of her hair.

Suddenly, her head swung to him. Mortals couldn't see as well as dragons in the dark, but he could've sworn her gaze met his. He blinked, stunned by the direct eye contact and the unusual, lavender eyes.

He frowned, wondering if he had seen eyes that color before. Something told him he had, but he didn't have time to search his memories when there was a trespasser to take care of.

Then, with slow, deliberate movements, she lowered her head covering to reveal long, thick tresses as black as the night sky.

Erith hoped she wasn't making a mistake. After her first encounter with Constantine, she had thought her curiosity over the immortal would be satisfied. But it wasn't. In fact, the longer she watched the King of Dragon Kings and his brethren, the more they fascinated her.

The Dragon Kings were honorable, noble, and principled. They didn't allow their significant and vast magical power to influence them as it did the Fae more times than not.

What made the Kings different? Why were they able to remain so...decent?

She met Con's gaze. It was no accident that she was here at this time. She'd watched his routine for the past few weeks and knew he took a nightly walk before he shifted and took to the skies.

Would he remember her? There was a chance. It had only been a hundred and forty-five years since she'd last spoken with him. Immortals might recall things like that, or forget them easily. She wasn't ready for him to put the pieces of her identity together. And she might never be.

There was a part of her that knew she should use glamour to alter her appearance just to be safe. But she didn't. It was a huge chance. But one she had to take. If he recognized her, then she would tell him who she was.

If.

Did she want him to recognize her? Did she want to tell him who she was?

Con walked to the edge of the stream, his boots coming within inches of the water. She lifted her chin and met his eyes. His face was in shadows, hidden by the sliver of moon and the clouds that drifted swiftly across the sky.

She liked that he was in a kilt. The plaid wasn't one seen anywhere else in Scotland. Actually, it wasn't seen outside of Dreagan. The tartan was one designed and crafted by the Dragon Kings specifically for them.

It was a bold mix of various colors on a black base. Yet it worked beautifully. Every Dragon King was represented in the tartan. The plaid was as wild as the Highlands and as fierce as the Kings themselves.

"Who are you?"

"Iris," she told him, using one of the many flower names that she so loved. Erith held her breath as Con's stare became intense.

He walked into the stream, uncaring that the water came nearly to his knees, soaking his boots. Con didn't stop until he reached the opposite bank to stand before her. "You're on private land."

"The woods called to me." That wasn't a lie. Every magical being on the realm felt the pulse of magic on Dreagan.

"You can no' be here."

This Con was much changed from than the one she'd spoken with before. This Con was colder, more aloof. More...isolated. She'd seen it in him the last time, but once they spoke, he had lowered his walls a little.

Not this time, however. The walls were reinforced several times over.

That made her sad. She wanted to warn him, to caution him on keeping hope alive. It was that optimism which would sustain the Kings for millennia to come. But she couldn't blame him for how he felt.

He'd been born to the skies. Now, he and the others were reduced to hiding not just themselves but also their magic. A hundred years of that was enough to make anyone go mad. And the Dragon Kings had endured for countless eons.

No, they had suffered.

Such majestic, commanding creatures shouldn't be subjected to such atrocities. It broke her heart. She longed to reach out to Con and tell him...what? What would she tell him?

That she understood because she was also immortal? Or should she tell him that everything would work out in the end? She couldn't see the future. She had no idea what would happen. She only knew that the Dragon Kings needed to survive no matter what.

Obviously, she'd made a mistake thinking she could come to Con again. Perhaps if she had said her name was Heather, but no. That wouldn't work either. He would demand to know why he hadn't been able to find her. And she'd have to tell him.

Death bowed her head, defeated and sad. "Then I shall go."

She turned and took two steps when Con said, "Stop,"

Erith stilled, the soft crunch of his boots

on the graveled dirt growing louder as he walked closer. She felt movement to her left, her eyes darting in that direction as Constantine came to stand before her once more.

"Who are you?" he demanded again.

Her heart thudded. Did he recognize her? It wasn't too late for her to use glamour. The night and its shadows helped to hide any number of things. Then again, a Dragon King was looking at her. A dragon with eyesight sharper than any other, one that was able to see in the night as well as they did in the day.

The color of her eyes was distinctive. That could be the very thing that caused him to remember.

"Iris," she repeated.

A small frown furrowed his brow. "Iris."

A soft breeze floated around them, ruffling his blond waves pulled back at his neck and causing a lock to come free from the rest and fall into his eyes. He blinked, seemingly unbothered by the hair tangled in his lashes.

"And you are?" she asked, needing to keep up the ruse.

Whenever she finally told Con the truth—

however long until that time, because she *would* tell him—he would be furious that she had deceived him. Hopefully, he would allow her to explain why she had taken such action.

"Constantine," he replied after a long, silence. "Are you lost?"

"Nay. I wanted to see the woods."

He glanced over her shoulder to the trees. "They called to you, you say."

"Aye."

"You're no' from Scotland."

Erith decided to tell some of the truth, but she would have to tread carefully. Con was the type of man who would latch on to something he wanted to know and not give up until he'd secured it. And she very much wanted to talk to him again. "I'm not from anywhere."

"Everyone is from somewhere."

She grinned. "Or everywhere. I travel."

"Alone?" he asked, a brow quirked.

Erith bit back a smile since his reaction was similar to their first meeting. "I never said I was alone."

"You are now."

"So are you."

He narrowed his eyes slightly. Without uttering a word, she sensed his doubt about her.

She glanced over her shoulder at the trees. "This is a beautiful place. Treasure it."

"Are you a Druid?" he asked, stepping to the side to stop her from leaving.

"Nay."

His head tilted to the side slightly. "Fae?"

Erith swallowed, becoming nervous. "Nay."

"But you felt the magic?" he asked with a hard look.

"I said the woods called to me. I never spoke of magic."

He crossed his arms over his wide chest and pinned her with a stare, his arm muscles stretching the fabric of his shirt. "You talk of magic calmly, like someone who knows no' only what it is but how to use it. If you didna have any, you would act like all the others and become outraged with fear at such talk."

"I've seen magic." Once more, she found herself toeing the line between truth and fiction.

No matter how much she wanted to tell Con who she was, now wasn't the time. She'd felt a connection with the King of Dragon Kings the first time she saw him. She believed it was because he was the leader of such a powerful group of beings.

On and off throughout the passage of time, she looked in on him, curious as to how he was doing. He was the one who held everything together at Dreagan. She didn't think any of the other Kings even realized how hard Con worked—or the lengths he'd gone to for them.

The sacrifices he made.

The more she'd seen, the more she'd wanted to know Con. She'd taken that chance a century and a half ago, and it had confirmed what she already suspected—Con was someone she wanted as an ally.

A friend.

And yet, something stopped her each time she tried to tell him who she was. Not because he wouldn't welcome her. Because of her past. There were things she never wanted to think about again. Things too...horrible to admit.

She couldn't get the words out again this time for fear of his disdain. Yet she knew that their paths were destined to intertwine again. Maybe then she would be able to tell him who she was. Maybe then....

"You've seen magic?" he repeated softly,

his face going blank. "How? When? By who?"

"Would you believe anything I tell you?"

"Nay," he replied. "You're lying to me, and I doona know why."

She put her hand into the pocket of her skirt and wrapped her fingers around the gift she'd brought. The metal was cool against her palm, and she worried that he might disregard anything she gave him.

So she decided to change the subject.

"Are you one of them?" she asked.

He blinked. "One of who?"

"The dragons," she said, pointing over her shoulder.

Erith inwardly smiled when a frown flashed quickly over his face. The unflappable Con was rattled.

His gaze darted to the sky before they slid back to her, waiting.

"Aye, I saw them," she told him. "I gather you're not pleased by that."

"I'm no', but that can be remedied."

"I'm one woman. What harm can I do to you?"

He dropped his arms. "You could destroy everything."

"Do you not trust anyone?"

"No' those I doona know."

She turned toward the water and sat. "That's rather...sad. Life is about taking chances."

"And you know about that?"

"Rather a lot, actually," she admitted.

Silence filled the air. She didn't look at him, but it took everything she had to keep her head forward and not see what Con was doing—or thinking. Not that he showed anything—ever—but there was always a chance of glimpsing something.

"I should have your memories wiped, and you escorted off our land," he stated.

She pulled her legs to her chest and rested her chin on her knees. "That is your right. Or...you could sit and talk to me."

"Why?"

Erith shrugged. "Why not?"

Once more, he fell silent. She listened to the water trickling downriver while a fox screamed in the distance. An owl swooped from the trees, catching a mouse in its talons before flying off.

Finally, Con moved to stand beside her. Then, after another hesitation, he sat. "Do I know you?"

Yes. "Wouldn't I have told you if you

did?" Death swallowed the bite of her lie. "I know why you hide here. It's a stunning place to disappear, but you should find a way to get out among others."

"Why?"

"Because they will find you eventually. You should be the one to set the rules, not them." She turned her head to look at him. He was immortal, but the weight of responsibility, the lines of worry were there in the set of his mouth and the tone of his words. "Find a way to interact with the rest of the world while keeping your privacy."

He let out a snort. "That's impossible."

"It's not. You just haven't found the right thing yet. You like control. Take it."

Con leaned back on his hands and stretched out his legs before him. "You talk as if you know all about me."

"Who says I don't?" she replied with a smile.

He didn't return it as his gaze met hers. "Who are you?"

"A friend who the trees called to. A friend who marvels at the dragons soaring in the clouds. A friend who wishes to help."

"A friend I doona know," he replied

softly.

Too softly. He was angry and troubled. Not a good combination for anyone, but especially dangerous when it came to a Dragon King.

She lifted her face to the sky. "Trust is a precarious thing. Some give it freely, while others hold it tightly to their chests. Those who are stingy are never rewarded."

"I know just how prickly trust is," he stated, his words clipped. "I've felt the cold blade of betrayal, and it isna something one recovers from."

Erith wondered if Con realized that, even now, his anger wasn't directed at Ulrik, it was because his friend had been so viciously deceived. Con hurt *for* his friend. Because the betrayal he spoke of had been done to only one Dragon King—Ulrik.

"Time heals all things." She looked at him, wishing she could see his black eyes that faded into the night. "It heals treachery, friendships. And love."

That one word made Con stiffen. It was so slight, she would've missed it had she not been looking.

"Time means nothing to me," he replied.

"Everyone measures time. Some in

moments, some in years, and some in centuries. But it is a part of life."

He looked away. "How do you measure it?"

Damn. She hadn't thought about him asking her that. "By eras of my own choosing."

"So you doona conform?"

"Why should I? The ones who say to act a certain way make up the rules to curtail others. Everyone has an inner code. They know right and wrong."

Con rolled onto his side toward her, propped up by one elbow as he regarded her. "But no' everyone can distinguish between right and wrong."

"That's true, but do the laws put in place help them choose? Nay. All they do is tell them what they're doing is wrong—which they know anyway—and what punishment they'll receive."

For the first time, there was a hint of a smile on Con's face. "Verra true."

"You know the man you are," she said. "You know your obligations and duties. You know what needs to be done, and you do it."

"How do you ken that?"

She wanted to kick herself. She'd gotten carried away by their talk and was now paying the price for revealing too much. But she needed a friend. "I see it in your eyes. Even the way you approached me. But it was the fact that you didn't throw me off your land that told me everything else."

"How do you know I willna toss you on your arse?"

Erith smiled. "Because you sat to talk to me."

"Con? Is the intruder taken care of?"

He wanted to ignore Royden, but he knew if he didn't, it would bring others to him, and he didn't want that. In fact, Con was quite content to be alone with the beautiful stranger. "*Everything is fine,*" he answered.

Iris. Without comprehending how, he knew the name wasn't hers. There was something about her that was familiar. The easy way they spoke should worry him, as if they were long-lost friends. But he would remember someone like her.

She was utterly unforgettable. Not only because of her beauty, but also because of the gentleness that somehow went hand-in-hand with her spine of steel.

He should've removed her from Dreagan immediately, but something, some unknown force he couldn't name, stopped him. And once he began talking to Iris, he couldn't seem to stop.

A blind man would have been able to see

that she held a wealth of secrets, but not once did he believe that she was there to do any harm to him or the other Kings. While she managed to evade his questions for the most part, he wasn't angry. Just...continually curious.

"Will you walk with me?"

Her question took him off guard. Then again, everything she did surprised him. Con quite liked their spot near the stream, but he found himself saying, "Aye," before he knew what was happening.

She gave him a dazzling smile and rose to her feet in one fluid motion. He stood and looked down at her, noting that she barely came to his shoulders. A sudden, inescapable need to protect her rose within him.

Her eyes blinked up at him, clear and sincere. In the moonlight, the lavender orbs had a fire unto themselves. A Druid she wasn't. He suspected she was a Fae who used glamour to hide herself.

Iris turned, her long, black hair swinging with her. She lifted her skirts and crossed the stream at its narrowest point and made her way into the thick trees. He followed a step behind her, still attempting to figure out why she was there.

"Why did you speak of hope?" he asked.

She stopped beside a small, creeping shrub. It wasn't until she bent to smell the fragrant, delicate bloom that he realized what it was. A twinflower. Iris's touch was gentle as she looked closely at the pinkish-white, downward-facing, bell-shaped flowers. He'd always found the little plants with their five-petaled flowers hanging on either side of a forked stem unique and quite pretty.

Irish whispered something to the plant before she straightened and briefly met his gaze before continuing on. "Hope is what helps things continue. You're losing yours."

He didn't dispute her claim. "It's a wasted emotion."

"Why do you say that?"

"From my experience, it only sets you up for disappointment."

Iris stopped and turned to him. "All of your experience? There isn't one instance where hope gave you something in return?"

Con looked away from her probing gaze. It was as if she could see straight into his soul, into the dark corners where he kept his most private desires and yearnings.

"It takes someone with great strength to

have hope," Iris continued. "There is nothing about you that appears weak. Giving up. Well, that's what a timid man does."

His gaze slid back to her. "Complimenting me now?"

"Maybe." Her smile was slow. "I don't think you get enough of that."

"Speaking once more as if you know me."

She shrugged and turned to continue walking. Her hands brushed every tree and plant she passed as she made her way through the Dragonwood. To his amazement, animals drew near her as if summoned by some silent decree.

He was positive she was Light Fae.

"Why do you no' want me to know who you are?" he asked.

"Why does it have to matter? I come as a friend."

"Because I think you came for a reason."

She stopped again. This time, there were several beats of silence before she turned to him. "And if I did?"

"I want to know why?"

"I came to see you."

He raised a brow. "Why?"

"To get to know you."

It was one of the few times where he

believed she told the truth. "Did someone send you?"

She shook her head and smiled softly. "I came on my own." Her head fell back to look at the limbs of the trees towering over her. "This place is amazing. You're lucky to have it."

"Do you have something similar?"

"Aye." She looked at him once more. "Everyone should have such a place. The peace it offers is infinite. I think it also gives us shelter when we might not even realize we need it."

He leaned a shoulder against an oak that was over five hundred years old. "The entire time you've been here, I've gotten the feeling that you're trying to impart some kind of lesson."

"Perhaps," she replied. "Maybe I'm just lonely and want someone to talk to about things that I've been thinking about."

"Do you no' have anyone?"

She glanced away but not before he saw the stark loneliness in her expression. "Not really. There are others, but...."

Her words trailed off, and he waited for her to finish. When she didn't, he said, "But, sometimes, you can't talk to them because you doona want to worry them. Or it's as simple as you can no' tell them."

"Exactly," she said with a slight curve of her lips. "That's precisely it. Do you have any advice?"

"Find someone you can talk to."

Her smile widened. "I think I just did. Will you be my friend, Con?"

He didn't hesitate to reply, "Aye. Does this mean you'll tell me who you really are?"

"I'm your friend. Can't we let that be enough for now?"

Con bowed his head because he knew he would get nothing else from her then. Perhaps the next time they met.

"Do you have someone you can talk to?" she asked.

He met her gaze. "You?"

"Is that a question?" she asked with a laugh. "Of course, you can talk to me."

"But can I trust you?"

Her smile died as she stared into his eyes. "I vow on my life that you can."

He wanted to believe her, but how could he when he knew she lied? Though he enjoyed talking with her, he wouldn't share his secrets. But she was a welcome distraction. Perhaps if their friendship progressed, she might earn his trust, and then he might open up to her.

"I'll prove it to you one day," she said as if reading his thoughts.

"Why is it so important?"

She shrugged and turned her head away to look at two foxes playing. "I just have a feeling that we're meant to be friends. I think one day, we may need each other."

Her words made him rethink the Druid part. "You can see the future?"

"Nay," she replied softly. "Even if I could, I don't think I would. Knowing makes things worse."

"Or it would allow for different decisions."

Her head swiveled back to him. "How would you ever know if you changed anything? What if seeing the future and making a different decision is exactly why you were shown the future?"

"I doona know," he replied with a shrug. "It gets confusing."

Con pushed away from the tree and took a few steps closer to her. "Where do you live?"

"Far from here."

"You willna tell me?"

Sadness filled her face. "Not now."

"Do you no' trust me?"

Her eyes widened. "Of course, I do."

"Then tell me."

Her large eyes closed as she sighed and shook her head. "It isn't that simple. I want to tell you, and I will." Her eyes opened, spearing him with an intense look. "Just not today."

"I should remove you from Dreagan. I know it. Just as I know that I shouldna be talking to you."

"I'm glad you haven't. And I'm really glad we are speaking. It's not easy for me to say that I need to talk."

"You could've chosen anyone. Why me?"

Her lips suddenly curved into a smile. "You're the King of Dragon Kings. Only you would understand."

With a few words, she'd revealed something very important about herself. If only he could relate to her, then that meant she was in a position of power much like he was. He didn't know any Fae like that, but in truth, he didn't make it his business to learn anything about the Fae. Maybe he should.

He wanted to know who Iris really was—including her real name. Mostly, because he didn't like being lied to for any reason. But...he liked the idea of having a friend. If she were Fae, he wouldn't tell her any secrets of the Dragon Kings, but sometimes talking didn't mean secrets were involved. Sometimes, it just meant knowing that someone was there for you.

He'd had that in his life. Twice. Once with Ulrik. And then with...

Not that the other Kings weren't his friends. They were, but the only one who truly knew what was going on was Kellan since he was the Keeper of History. Since Kellan held so many secrets from all the Kings, Con didn't want to add to that. That was why it was easier to just keep everything to himself and his journal.

"Sometimes your sadness swallows you."

His gaze snapped to Iris.

She watched him. "It eats away at you. And now, it's threatening to envelop you. Who are you thinking about to bring on such desolation?"

"I'm thinking of the past."

"Aye. But one person in particular."

He shook his head, not wanting to talk about it. "Shall we walk some more?"

"Is that what you do to dispel the memories?"

"Nay," he said as they walked side by side. "They're always there. I simply refuse to let them out."

She made a sound in the back of her throat. "But they come out anyway. When you sleep."

That's exactly what happened, which was why he rarely slept.

And never fell into dragon sleep.

If he did, the pain he kept at bay would engulf him. If that happened, he wasn't sure he'd ever come back from it. He'd learned to mask his feelings, and it helped him get through many hardships. Because if he gave in, if he allowed himself to feel even a little, then he'd be swarmed by a tidal wave of emotions.

The repercussions of that weren't something he even wanted to think about.

"Have you ever been in love?" he asked.

Iris acted as though the question didn't bother her, but Con saw the rapid beat of her pulse at her throat. She didn't even look his way, just kept walking.

Finally, after another few minutes, she said, "Love is dangerous."

"I can no' deny that, but you didna answer my question, lass."

Her gaze took on a faraway look. "Love isn't really an option for me."

"Again, you didna answer."

She sighed softly. Then, in the softest whisper, she said, "Aye."

"What happened?"

Iris's feet halted, but she still didn't look his way. "I may not be able to control my heart or the feelings stirred within it, but I can make certain I don't act on it."

"So the person doesna know." Somehow, he'd expected Iris to be the kind of woman who would slay anything and anyone who got between her and love.

"They do not. Nor will they ever."

"Can I ask why?" Con pressed.

Her lips pressed together before her lavender eyes swung to him. "Love isn't something I can have."

"Why no'?"

She faced him and quirked a brow, her gaze harsh. "How about you, Con? Have you loved? I can see that you have. Deeply.

Where is she?"

"Far enough away that I can never have her." When Iris kept staring at him, he blew out a breath. "Because love isna something I can have. Point taken."

Iris licked her lips and briefly looked at the ground. "We both have our reasons for keeping our hearts locked away. Others wouldn't understand or accept our motives, but then again, they aren't in our positions, are they?"

"Nay," he replied in a whisper.

She suddenly issued a soft chuckle. "Time is a funny thing. It sometimes feels as if we have too much of it. Then on other occasions, there is never enough."

He knew without having to ask that she was leaving. And that made him very sad. "Will you come again?"

"Yes," she said with a smile.

"I look forward to it."

She put her hand on his arm. "Don't give up on hope, and remember, the Dragon Kings control their own destinies."

He watched her walk away. After she was about twenty feet away, he said, "I'll always be here if you need to talk."

Iris turned to him and smiled. "Until next

time, King of Kings." Then she disappeared.

Con shook his head with a smile. A Fae. Just as he'd suspected.

He stared at the spot for several minutes, then walked from the Dragonwood and shifted. He spread his wings and took to the skies, Iris's words running through his mind.

When dawn broke, he returned to Dreagan Mountain. He shifted to his human form and dressed, lovingly folding the tartan into pleats before lying on top of the material to put it on.

He made his way to his office, intending to make another journal entry and drawing of Iris. As he entered the chamber, he saw a leather pouch on the desk with a folded piece of parchment leaning against it.

Con lifted the letter and looked at the wax seal. He'd never seen such a symbol before. It was a circled triskelion inside a triangle. He cracked the wax and unfolded the parchment.

Constantine –

I wish we had more time, but what little I got to spend with you is something I'll treasure forever. It's always time that seems to rule us in one way or another. Don't let it govern you.

While there is much I didn't tell you, please understand that it had nothing to do with you and everything to do with me. I sincerely hope that we will be friends because I think we both need one. I planned our meeting for some weeks. I wish I had given this to you in person, but I've learned that sometimes it's better to do it this way.

Time can be a friend as well as an enemy. My gift will let you move about as you wish.

Hold onto hope with all that you are.

Your friend,
Iris

Con read the letter twice more before he gently set it down and pulled his chair out, his gaze landed on the leather pouch. He sat and placed his hands on either side of the gift, staring at it.

His curiosity finally won, and he reached for it. He was mildly surprised at its weight. After unwrapping the leather around it, he tugged the opening wide and peered inside.

Slowly, he dipped his hand into the bag and wrapped his fingers around the round, metal object. He brought it out and stared at the gold pocket watch. On the cover, engraved into the metal, were two dragon heads, facing away from each other.

The body of the watch had beautiful Celtic knotwork wound around it. The back had a small flower etched into the center. An iris. He smiled as he ran his thumb over it.

Con turned the watch back over and pressed the latch to open it. His lips parted at the beauty before him. It wasn't a typical timepiece of the mortals. It was one crafted just for him.

The inside was made of onyx with a portion opened to see the gold gears turning. There was a tiny gold dragon at the top. He watched the movement of the gears for several moments before he realized what it was tuned to—magic.

With a smile, he set the watch aside, leaving it open to look at it. Then he reached for his journal. For the next forty minutes, he meticulously drew Iris as he'd first seen her standing by the stream after she removed the head covering.

The 21st of April, human year 1746

After all this time, I should be prepared for surprises. And yet, oddly, I never am. I suppose I get stuck in the daily life we now lead as humans. Then, every so often, something special happens.

Today, it came in the form of a Fae named Iris. It's not her real name, but that doesn't matter. It should, I know it should, and it might later, but right now, it doesn't. She came when I needed a friend the most. And it seems she needed one, as well.

She spoke of hope and time. Two things I don't think about often. Time will move as it always has. And hope, well, I've not had any in quite some time. Iris has made me rethink a few things.

Specifically, she brought up something I've

long worried about—humans wanting to invade Dreagan. Our magic has kept them out this long, but the more of them there are, the more they'll want to know about our home.

Iris suggested that we decide how that will happen. She's right. It's something we should've been preparing for starting many years ago, but it isn't too late. We need something that will put us front and center in their world while allowing us to continue hiding.

Con picked up the pocket watch and closed it, rubbing his thumb over the double dragon etching. He set it down and went back to his journal.

Whatever we decide on, it's going to have to be perfect. Otherwise, I don't know what will become of us. What I do know is that for the first time in days, months, years, I'm actually looking forward to something. We need a plan. That's something I can focus on, but most importantly, it's something that I can make right for us.

I'm not sure when I'll see Iris again. I hope it's sooner rather than later. I'd like to thank her for the gift. As well as figure out her cryptic message about it allowing me to move about as I want. However, I also wish to talk to her again. It was a pleasant time. I can see the loneliness within her, but I believe that's because I have it myself.

I've been leery of the Light Fae for some time, especially since the queen, Usaeil, continues to want to befriend me. I'm unsure of her motives. I'll continue to be cautious with her, but perhaps I should strengthen the alliance between the dragons and Light Fae. I might then be able to find out about Iris.

I will add that I don't think Iris is Dark Fae. I could be wrong. But I really hope I'm not.

Constantine, the King of Golds
King of Dragon Kings

Con closed the journal and put the pocket watch in his sporran. As he rose to his feet, he glanced at the sideboard where bottles of wine sat. It was too bad Scotland didn't have its own kind of liquor, something that would be distinctly theirs.

He stilled as he thought about the experiment some of the Dragon Kings had been conducting over the last several decades. Con strode from his office and out the manor to a building where others had been distilling whisky for over two hundred years.

Varek and Merrill gave a nod when they saw him.

"Con," Merrill said.

He strode to the large vat they had built and stood before it with his arms crossed. "How is this coming?"

Varek shrugged, grinning. "Pretty good."

Con peered into the container. He knew from his own tastings of their attempts that it was good. Really good.

Merrill rose from his stool and motioned to a stack of casks. "We discovered that the longer we leave the whisky in the barrels, the better it tastes."

Varek snorted. "That's because Keltan forgot about a couple of barrels that we had when we began this. He opened one accidentally, and it was so good, we finished it off ourselves."

The more they talked, the more a plan began to form in Con's mind. Then he tasted the liquor. He had three more glasses, each time, more of his idea sliding into place.

Con grinned and held up his now empty glass. "Tell me you've perfected the recipe."

"Aye," they replied in unison.

"Good," Con said. "Because this is going to be how we live among the humans."

Varek frowned. "Is that a good idea?"

"We'll have to eventually," Merrill said. His gaze shifted to Con. "I like this. What are we going to call our whisky?"

Con thought of the pocket watch and the design. "Dreagan."

"Gaelic for dragon," Varek said with a smile. "The mortals willna realize what we're hiding."

"And our logo will be a double dragon head," Con declared. "Get things moving, my friends, to make more of this. I'll tell the others. I doona want to be the first to sell because of the attention that would shine on us, but we will be the best."

Con left the building, his steps lighter than they had been in a very long time. He had a plan thanks to Iris. And it was going to be the very thing that gave them everything they needed to live amongst the humans.

Death

Erith smiled as she strolled among her flowers. As she meandered through the heady scents, her clothes faded to be replaced by a black gown with a full skirt that fell into a train behind her. Her realm was to her what the Dragonwood was to Con. But she couldn't remain for long. There was work to be done.

She walked to the white tower that was her home and took her place in a chamber. When she was with Con, she could be Erith, but back on her realm, she was Death. And it was time for her to be judge and jury to the Fae.

After she'd done her duty, she set the robins out to give Cael her decisions. Cael and the other Reapers would carry out the executions. Except she didn't want to be alone. Maybe it was her talk with Con, but she didn't want to be by herself.

Erith couldn't decide on a location. But

there was one who drew her thoughts again and again. It was folly to give into the temptation, but she couldn't seem to tell her heart no.

Before she knew it, she stood in the area claimed by the Reapers. It was empty, but then again, she had expected that. It was the only reason she had come. It wasn't that she didn't like her Reapers. Quite the opposite. They were each fierce warriors, and in many ways, her family.

But to deliver her decisions herself meant that she had to interact with Cael often. So, she used the robins.

She stilled. Someone was behind her. She knew without looking who it was. Cael. The very one she didn't want to see. But she couldn't ignore him. She turned to face the Light Fae, meeting his silver eyes.

"Erith," he said.

The deep, rich timbre of his Irish brogue was enough to make her heart skip a beat. "Cael."

"I didn't expect you."

"I didn't intend a visit."

One side of his lips quirked up. "Checking up on me?"

"I don't doubt your ability to lead. I never

have."

He blinked, the smile gone as he grew serious. "Are you all right?"

"I'm Death. No one worries about me."

~ ~ ~

Cael blinked, and Erith vanished. He sighed and said, "I do. I always will."

THANK YOU

Thank you for reading **CONSTANTINE: A History Part 2**. I hope seeing into the past and discovering how the Dragon Kings began distilling whisky—and getting the symbol—allowed you more insight into Con.

Please read on for an excerpt from **DARK ALPHA'S EMBRACE**, the second Reaper book. You will find buy links to the entire Dark World at the end.

If you've not checked out my new www.MotherOfDragonsBooks.com website, please do. It's all things dragons and the Dark World. You can find the reading order, characters listed by Dragon Kings, Reapers, Fae, humans, and Druid, places, and things found in each of the series.

Donna Grant

www.DonnaGrant.com
www.MotherofDragonsBooks.com

DARK ALPHA'S EMBRACE

The Reapers Series, Book 2

Edinburgh, Scotland
New Year's Eve

Kyran stared curiously at the large gray structure of Edinburgh's Central Library. What was it about such places that called to some mortals? Even the half-Fae Jordyn found it one of the most amazing places in the city.

He didn't get it.

"Just a building full of books," Kyran mumbled.

Talin smacked him in the arm as he came to stand beside Kyran. "Don't knock it. Many of the books on Jordyn's list are in that place. The more she has, the more information we get."

"I know." That didn't mean he liked it.

Talin turned his silver eyes to him. "What's the problem?"

Kyran shot him a look. "We're Fae, Talin. Reapers. We kill those Death chooses. We don't break into libraries and take books. Our skills are being wasted."

"It's a change, that's for sure." Talin chuckled softly and rubbed his hands together. "I attempted to check out one of the books on Jordyn's list, but the librarian is fierce. She told me I was asking about a book in the ancient section, as if I was supposed to know what that meant."

Kyran rubbed his eyes with his thumb and forefinger. He'd already heard this story four times, and each time the librarian became more and more ferocious. "Aye."

"When I asked what that was, she looked at me as if I'd grown another head. Then she said, in that uptight tone of hers, 'You're Irish.' As if that makes a difference."

"I told you to get a human to ask for them."

With a snort, Talin ran his hands through his long black hair. "We're getting the books tonight. What difference does it make?"

"Why can't we just use magic and find them someplace else?"

Talin rolled his eyes. "Did you not listen to Jordyn when she briefed us on this? These books are extremely rare. There is only one edition for each."

"And some just happen to be in this library?" No, Kyran wasn't buying it. "Why this place?"

Talin looked around, his hands held out. "We're in Edinburgh. It's one of the oldest cities. Where else would these books be?"

"Private owners."

"Let it go," Talin said with a shake of his head.

But Kyran didn't want to let it go. Why did he have to get stuck with the library instead of going to some of the private collectors? He'd much rather do that than sneak around a building.

There was no adventure in it. They'd be in and gone without anything happening.

"The library closed at eight," Talin said. "It's after midnight now. We'll have the books in hand and return to Jordyn in a blink."

"That's the problem. There's no danger."

"Ah. I see." Talin walked backward into the middle of the narrow street that was empty of people and cars. "You want danger? We'll get it as soon as we get the books. Then we can locate Bran."

The anger within Kyran sizzled at the

mention of the ex-Reaper. Bran betrayed his group and was sent to the Netherworld by Death.

Except Bran managed to escape the inescapable prison and was now after them. Bran had already killed Jordyn in his bid to take the Reapers out.

But Death stepped in and made Jordyn one of them. Though she was a Reaper—the first female Reaper—Jordyn didn't assassinate as they did.

Her job was coordinating everything, as well as research. Jordyn's first order of business was discovering all she could about the Netherworld.

Kyran couldn't wait to find Bran. Con and Eoghan might be the only ones who survived from the first group of Reapers, but Kyran would be the one to help take Bran down for good.

"Let's get going then," Kyran said.

With a wink, Talin veiled himself. Kyran watched the Light Fae and tried not to laugh. They'd become friends immediately, which still shocked Kyran since he was a Dark Fae.

Then again, each Reaper suffered some kind of betrayal in one form or another. That's what drew them all together, what bonded them. The seven of them only had each other. Well, they were eight now.

Kyran veiled himself so no human—or Fae—could see him. All Fae had the ability to veil themselves, but most could only hold it for a minute or so. Only the Reapers could remain that way indefinitely. It was one of the gifts of accepting Death's offer.

He walked across the street and up the steps to the main entrance to the library. It was locked and barred, which kept out the majority of the humans.

Kyran lifted his head to the cameras placed around the building. Some were in plain sight while others were hidden. The security system managed to keep out most of the criminals, but the mortals were resourceful when they really wanted something.

If the mortals knew of the books in the ancient section of the library and how much they were worth, no security system on the realm would keep the humans out.

But Kyran wasn't mortal. He teleported inside the library without a single hindrance. A long sigh fell from his lips. He was itching for a good fight ever since Bran got away a few weeks ago.

Death had been oddly quiet. There had been no assignments, and they were all growing restless. Except for Daire. The bastard was trailing a Light Fae Death wanted information on—Rhi. Kyran had no idea where Daire was. He only hoped Daire was having more fun than he was.

They'd also not seen a glimpse of Cael since Death told him who helped Bran escape the Netherworld. Each of the Reapers wanted a piece of the Fae responsible for that, but Cael departed before anyone could go with him.

Kyran looked at the help desk standing in front of him where Talin had tried—unsuccessfully—to get one of the books from the library.

He unveiled himself, his magic keeping him hidden from the cameras as he strode to the stairs and descended to the next level. Talin decided to come in from the roof and take the top three floors while Kyran searched the bottom.

Talin bet him before they arrived that the books were stored in the top hidden floor of the library. Frankly, Kyran didn't care where they were as long as they found the books and left.

His hands itched to hold his sword. More than anything Kyran wanted to find Bran and sever his head from his body. It would go a long way in helping him feel better about being tracked by Bran and his Dark Fae army—and for what happened to Jordyn.

She and Baylon might be in love, but Kyran thought of her like a sister. As soon as that thought went through his mind, he inwardly cringed.

Even now, so many thousands of years later, the thought of his sister could make him feel as if he were being crushed on all sides. He hadn't been the only one betrayed that rainy night in Dublin.

There was never a good time for those memories to be brought into the light, but on the anniversary of the day he became a Reaper, Kyran allowed a few of those memories loose.

They never did him any good. They only served as a reminder, but it was one he needed. Because time had a way of making someone forget important facts. It was the mind's way of allowing a person to move on.

But Kyran didn't want to move on.

He reached the next floor and quickly went about searching rooms, hoping that behind every door would be the place he sought.

Kyran explored the next two floors but came up empty. Frustration soured his mood. He turned around and nearly ran into Talin who was standing behind him.

"You look vexed," Talin said. "Are you vexed, Kyran?"

For some odd reason, Talin was fixated on that word. He used it as often as he could, annoying everyone in the process. Kyran glared at him. "If I wasn't, I am now."

Talin's smile was wide. "Everyone should be vexed once in a while."

"Find another word," Kyran growled as he pushed past Talin.

Talin leaned a shoulder against the wall. "I didn't find a damn thing on my floors. I even double-checked the main level. Nothing. I know it's here."

"Aye, it's here. We just have to find it."

Pushing away from the wall, Talin stood and slowly turned in a circle. "We're missing it."

"It's hidden somehow."

"Not with magic."

Kyran eyed the books around him. "But maybe magic will help show it."

"And you thought this wouldn't be adventurous."

Kyran snorted. "If you think this is exciting, then we need to have a talk." Suddenly Talin moved to block him from walking away. Kyran lifted a brow. "Something on your mind?"

"Are you all right?"

"You mean besides wanting to find Bran? Aye."

Talin waved away his words. "We all want Bran. This is something else."

Kyran put his hand out and shoved at Talin's shoulder as he walked past. "Look on the left side of the room. I'll take the right."

"You haven't been the same since Baylon brought Jordyn into the group."

That stopped Kyran in his tracks. He turned and gawked at Talin. "What are you going on about?"

"Death changed the rules. Baylon wasn't killed for loving Jordyn, and now she's one of us."

"So?"

Talin ran a hand down his face. "Are you

lonely?"

"What the hell kind of question is that?"

"One that, as your friend, I'm asking you to answer."

Kyran stared at him a long time before he let out a deep breath. "When Death asked me to join the Reapers, I knew what the rules were. We tell no Fae who we are, or they die. We develop no attachments to humans or Fae so no one can be used against us. We leave all family and friends behind, letting them believe we're dead."

"You still haven't answered the question. That vexes me."

"I have the six of you. I have our assignments, doling out justice."

Talin folded his arms over his chest. "So you are lonely."

Each time that emotion threatened Kyran, he hastily shoved it away. "We're Reapers, gifted by Death with more power and magic than any other Fae. We don't have time to be lonely."

"Of course." Talin dropped his arms and turned away.

"You're lonely, aren't you?"

Talin halted. Without turning around he said, "Maybe."

"Just because Death allowed Jordyn to be a Reaper doesn't mean any of us will get that same privilege. Jordyn proved herself worthy."

"I know."

Kyran watched his friend walk away without another word. He'd known when Cael sent Talin undercover to the Light Fae court that something was going to happen.

Talin ended up wooing the daughter of an influential advisor to the queen, Usaeil. Kyran had warned Talin to remember that while at court, everything was a lie, but it seemed his friend had forgotten his advice.

Now with Baylon and Jordyn's romance condoned by Death, Talin had hope. Which was the worst thing for any of them. Hope was viciously and ruthlessly snatched from them when they were betrayed. Death gave them a purpose.

But even Kyran could admit to being a tad jealous of Baylon for having the one thing all of them thought would never happen—love.

Kyran pivoted and walked to the far wall. He was about to use his magic when he saw a door half hidden by a large bookshelf. He walked around the bookshelf and spotted the opening that was just large enough for the door.

He let out a whistle to Talin while staring at the keypad that unlocked the door.

"This is it," Talin said as he ran up and saw it.

Kyran put his hand over the keypad and loosed a pulse of magic.

...Continued in
Dark Alpha's Embrace
The Reapers Series, Book 2

STAY UP-TO-DATE

Sign up for Donna's newsletter!

tinyurl.com/DonnaGrantNews

Be the first to get notified of new releases and be eligible for special subscribers-only exclusive content and giveaways.
Sign up today!

ABOUT DONNA GRANT

New York Times and *USA Today* bestselling author Donna Grant has been praised for her "totally addictive" and "unique and sensual" stories. She's written more than seventy novels spanning multiple genres of romance including the bestselling Dark King stories. Her acclaimed series, Dark Warriors, feature a thrilling combination of Druids, primeval gods, and immortal Highlanders who are dark, dangerous, and irresistible. She lives with two children, a dog, and three cats in Texas.

CONNECT WITH DONNA GRANT ONLINE

www.DonnaGrant.com

www.MotherofDragonsBooks.com

Newsletter: tinyurl.com/DonnaGrantNews

Text Updates:

text DRAGONKING to 24587

Facebook: AuthorDonnaGrant

Facebook Reader Group:

http://bit.ly/DGGroupies

Twitter: donna_grant

Instagram: DGAuthor

Pinterest: DonnaGrant1

Bookbub: http://bit.ly/2siVQKK

Amazon: http://amzn.to/2f8xeP0

Goodreads: http://bit.ly/2vinVCD

Spotify Book Playlists:

http://bit.ly/donnagrant_author

Made in the USA
Lexington, KY
27 February 2019